SAM and CHARLIE

(AND SAM TOO)

at CAMP!

Leslie Kimmelman   *Illustrated by* William Owl

Albert Whitman & Company
Chicago, Illinois

Library of Congress Cataloging-in-Publication Data

Kimmelman, Leslie.
Sam and Charlie (and Sam too) at camp / Leslie Kimmelman ;
illustrated by William Owl.
pages cm
Summary: "Sam and Charlie spend a week at summer camp for the very first time
and learn some valuable lessons about nature and friendship"—Provided by publisher.
[1. Camps—Fiction. 2. Nature—Fiction. 3. Friendship—Fiction.
4. Jews—United States—Fiction.] I. Owl, William, illustrator. II. Title.
PZ7.K56493Sat 2015
[E]—dc23
2014034529

The design is by Jordan Kost.

For more information about Albert Whitman & Company,
visit our web site at www.albertwhitman.com.

To J.J., one of my most enthusiastic readers, and to his brothers, Sean and Zachary—L.K.

For Fran—W.O.

TABLE OF CONTENTS

In Hebrew, YOM means DAY.

Always be on the lookout for the presence of wonder.

—E. B. White

This is Charlie.

This is Sam. They are best friends and first-time sleepaway campers.

This is Charlie's sister, who is too little for camp. She is Sam Too.

YOM ONE

SUNDAY

"We're here!" Charlie exclaimed. "Our first time at overnight camp!"

"We're here," said Sam Too sadly. "Good-bye, Charlie."

Charlie gave her little sister a hug. "Good-bye for now."

She went to the girls' side of camp.

Her best friend and next-door neighbor, Sam, had already gone to the boys' side.

"Welcome to camp, Charlie," said Liz, the Girls Bunk 1 counselor. "You'll love it here." She strummed her guitar.

Charlie unpacked Floppy. She already felt homesick. Then she saw a letter from her family.

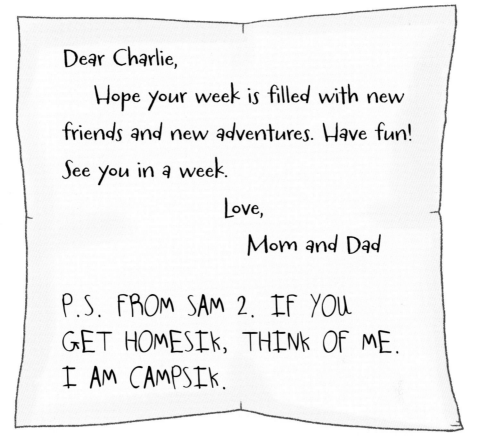

Dear Charlie,

Hope your week is filled with new friends and new adventures. Have fun! See you in a week.

Love,

Mom and Dad

P.S. FROM SAM 2. IF YOU GET HOMESIK, THINK OF ME. I AM CAMPSIK.

Charlie put on her bathing suit and climbed down from her bunk.

A girl named Olivia smiled at her.

"What's the name of this camp?" Liz was calling.

"Camp Morris!" everyone yelled.

"Well, yeah. But we call it Camp Get-Your-Feet-Wet. Which means camp is new for all of you, and we want you to have a great time. So, what's the name of this camp?"

"Camp Get-Your-Feet-Wet!" everyone yelled.

"Right!" said Liz. "So down to the lake to get your feet wet!"

Liz put one arm around Charlie. She put the other around Olivia.

And when they got to the lake, Sam was waiting.

MONDAY

Sam and Charlie were in the Dolphin group. They were allowed in the deep water.

Sam pretended to be a vampire squid.

Charlie pretended to be a scary, hairy sea monster.

"Cabin challenge!" the swim counselor
called. "Swim to Iceberg Rock and climb to
the top."

Swimming was easy. Sam and Charlie
took the lead.

Climbing up was harder.

At first, Charlie was faster.

"Are you going to let Bunk 1 beat you?" yelled Sam's bunkmates.

Soon Sam pulled ahead.

"Are you going to let Bunk 8 beat you?" yelled Charlie's bunkmates.

Sam and Charlie looked at each other... and reached the top together.

At the campfire that night, they got the "Camp Spirit" award.

TUESDAY

Sam wasn't fond of cabin clean-up.
His bunkmate Jackson liked it even less.

"Think of cabin clean-up as *shmirat ha'adamah*," suggested their counselor, Oren. "You know, taking care of the earth."

"And taking the earth *outside*," Sam said, sweeping.

A camper named Eli held up something squirmy. He said, "And taking the *earthworm* outside too."

Jackson s-l-o-w-l-y got to work.

Boys Bunk 8 took care of the earth— well, the dirt—*and* the earthworm. "But I still don't think we'll be getting the clean cabin award," said Sam, sweeping.

* * *

Back home, Sam Too's room was out of control. "When I come back, I don't want to see this mess," her mother warned.

14

And she didn't. Sam Too stuffed every-
thing under the bed, where her mother
couldn't see it.

WEDNESDAY

Charlie and her bunkmates were on a nature hike.

"I don't like nature," complained Caren.

"What does that even mean, you don't like it?" asked Olivia.

"Well, I don't like ants," Caren answered. "Eeuw—there's one!" She lifted her foot to stomp on it.

"Wait!" cried Charlie. She moved the ant away.

"Why did you do *that*?" Caren asked.

"You know—if you save one ant, it's like saving the entire world," said Charlie. "Maybe the colony can't get along without that ant. Maybe that ant is a really important ant."

They hiked on. Liz pointed out chip-
munks, rabbits, and a fantastic spiderweb.
Charlie saw an old beaver dam and a
couple of butterflies.

"Ow!" grumbled Caren. "A mosquito
stung me!" She wiped her forehead. "And
I'm hot. Hmph. Nature!"

"Almost there," said Liz.

They came to a small waterfall. Boys Bunk 8 was already there.

Sam cleared a space for Charlie. The other girls sat down too, and all the campers dangled their toes in the bubbly water. A breeze blew. A rainbow appeared in the misty air. Even Caren looked happy.

"Nature!" said Charlie, splashing Sam.

"Awesome!" agreed Sam, splashing back.

*** * ***

Sam Too was in the backyard. It had just stopped raining, and she'd caught a frog. Even better, a rainbow was forming overhead. "Do you think the other end of the rainbow is at Charlie's camp, Mom?"

THURSDAY

A fire truck pulled up on the field after breakfast. Its hose sprayed and sprayed— but it wasn't water that came out.

23

FRIDAY

All through breakfast, the rain came down.

"Blech," said Jackson. "I hate rain. Nothing to do."

It poured and roared all through cabin clean-up.

"Rain," said Charlie, sighing. "Just look at my hair. Frizz-city!"

Sam looked. *Whoa!* he thought. But he kept quiet. Charlie was sensitive about her hair.

It sploshed and sloshed all through morning activity.

Sam made seven lumpy lanyards. Charlie and Olivia made friendship bracelets and swapped them.

It flashed and crashed all through lunch. Charlie's hair got frizzier.

It whooshed and whirled all through afternoon activities.

There was a challah-making lesson.

Charlie had practice braiding Sam Too's hair, so braiding challah was easy-peasy.

Two loaves landed on the floor. Sam's loaf didn't rise. A boy named Larry ate raw dough and had to go to the nurse's office. Still, there were plenty of loaves for Shabbat dinner that night, an especially good meal served on snowy white tablecloths.

After the Sabbath prayers, Liz taught everyone camp songs, like "Boom Chicka Boom" and "John Jacob Jingleheimer Schmidt."

Then the campers went outside. The rain was slowing. It splattered and dripped and dropped and d-r-i-p-p-e-d and...stopped.

The sky was clear and starry.

Oren pointed. "Look! There's the Big Dipper!"

"Don't you mean the Big *Dripper*?" Charlie asked, cracking up.

The rainy day was over. The air smelled fresh. Shabbat peace was all around. And tomorrow was sure to be sunny again.

YOM SEVEN

SATURDAY

Shabbat was a day of rest at Camp Morris.

Everyone slept late. Then there was a Shabbat service.

After that, kids planned their own day.

"Look! I caught a grasshopper!" said Charlie. "Wanna touch?"

"No thanks," said Olivia, reading. "I'm at the most exciting part."

Sam went to Shabbat Tree House Hour, which was exactly what it sounded like— a one-hour Shabbat discussion in an amazing tree house. Even better than the one Sam had at home.

The day before, everyone had written c-mail—camp mail for other campers. Today it was delivered.

Sam got a c-mail from Charlie:

Hi Sam,

Camp was more fun because you were here. (But my challah looked better than yours!)

Your friend,

Charlie

Charlie got a c-mail from Sam:

Hi Charlie,
Foamy or muddy, you're still my buddy!

From,

Sam

Dinner was extra-tasty. Then the sun went down. So long, Shabbat.

The candle flames were out. The farewell campfire was on!

"Awesome week," said Sam.

"Camp-tastic!" agreed Charlie.

SUNDAY

There was one last "get-your-feet-wet" swim in the lake. One last breakfast. One last cabin clean-up.

Then good-byes were said, counselors thanked, and cars packed up. Campers and their families drove off.

"I like it better when you're around," Sam Too told Charlie in the car.

Charlie hugged her little sister. "Maybe *you'll* come to camp next summer."

"I hope so," said Sam Too. "I missed all the fun."

"Hmm," said Charlie. "I have an idea."

Back home that afternoon, Charlie and Sam and Sam Too had their own camp, Camp Bayit.

"That means *home* in Hebrew," Charlie explained.

They made friendship bracelets, sang camp songs, and squirted shaving foam until the cans were empty. And of course they stuffed themselves silly with s'mores.

"Camp Home is fun!" said Sam Too.

"Yeah, and you didn't even need to clean your room," said Sam.

"I will later," said Sam Too. "Counselor Mom said so."

THE END